TRUCKS
WHIZZ! ZOOM! RUMBLE!

by Patricia Hubbell
Illustrated by Megan Halsey

Marshall Cavendish • New York

For Marian Reiner—
with a truckload of thanks!
—P.H.

For Bill Hackett and Captain Bill—
for their trucks.
And for Sean—
for his map and his trucks
and everything else.
—M.H.

Text copyright © 2003 by Patricia Hubbell
Illustrations copyright © 2003 by Megan Halsey
All rights reserved.
Marshall Cavendish, 99 White Plains Road, Tarrytown, NY 10591
www.marshallcavendish.us
Library of Congress Cataloging-in-Publication Data
Hubbell, Patricia.
Trucks: whizz! zoom! rumble! / by Patricia
Hubbell ; illustrations by Megan Halsey.
p. cm.
Summary: A rhyming look at many different kinds of trucks, from
eighteen-wheelers to ice cream trucks, as they go about their business.
ISBN-13 978-0-7614-5124-2
ISBN 0-7614-5124-2
[1. Trucks—Fiction. 2. Stories in rhyme.] I. Halsey, Megan, ill. II. Title.
PZ8.3.H848 Wh 2003 [E]—dc21 2002008320

The text of this book is set in 24 point Italia medium.
The illustrations are rendered in collage.
Printed in Malaysia (T)
First edition

Old trucks.

New trucks.

Going-to-the-zoo trucks.

Red trucks.

Blue trucks.

Bringing-toys-to-you trucks.

Trailer trucks with lots of wheels.

Trucks that carry automobiles.

Trucks at rest stops getting gas,
whose drivers wave each time you pass.

Heavy trucks.

Light trucks... Whizzing-through-the-night trucks.

Garbage trucks.

Tow trucks.

Pack Mule Towing

Plowing-up-the-snow trucks

Arctic Plow Co.

Trucks that **RUMBLE**,

ROAR

and *shriek.*

Trucks that **putter**,

groan

and *creak.*

Trucks, trucks, trucks on the long, long road.

Ice-cream trucks.

Fire trucks.

Carpenters-for-hire trucks.

Dump trucks.

Tank trucks.

Going-to-the-bank trucks.

Trucks with horses.   Trucks with hens.

Trucks with big pink pigs in pens.

Tandem trucks
that go by twos.
Trucks that bring us
all the news.

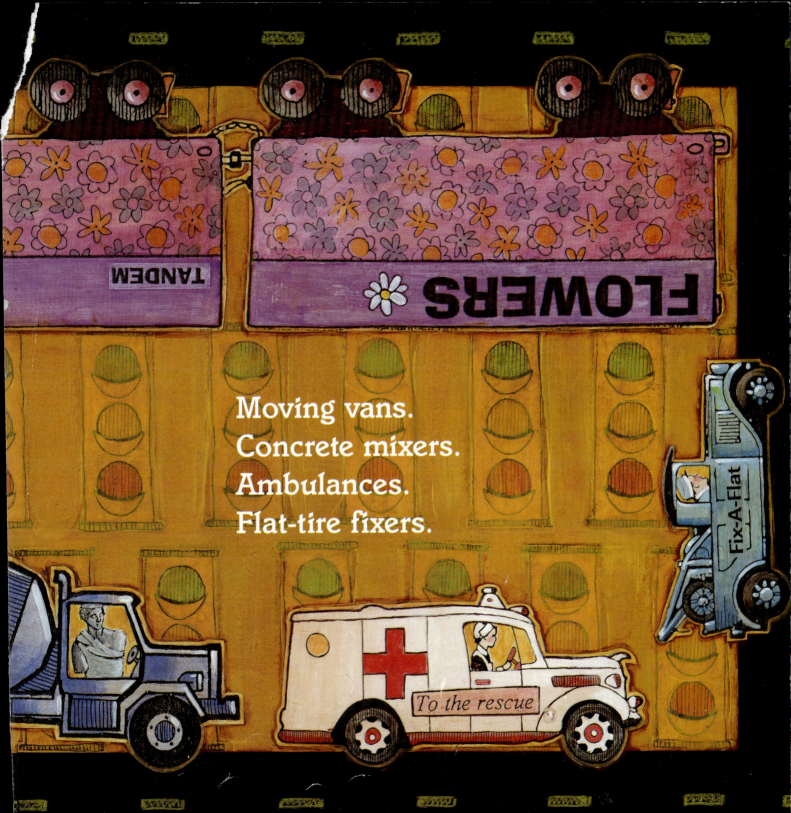

Moving vans.
Concrete mixers.
Ambulances.
Flat-tire fixers.

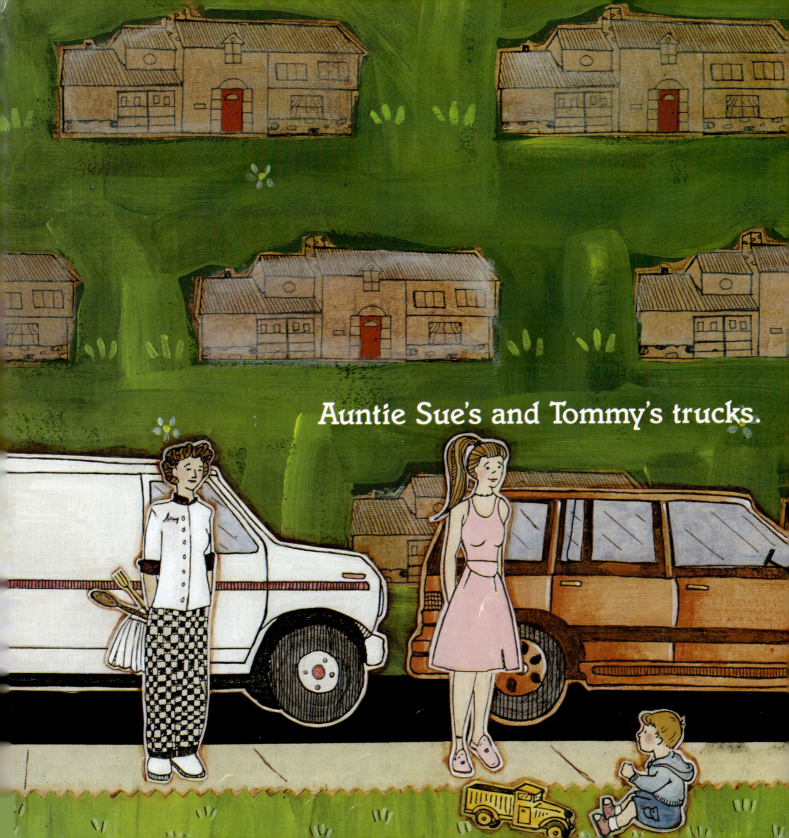

Auntie Sue's and Tommy's trucks.

Here you go in YOUR truck!

Zoom, zoom, zoom, down the long, long road.

Trucks go north, south, east and west.

They do their jobs.

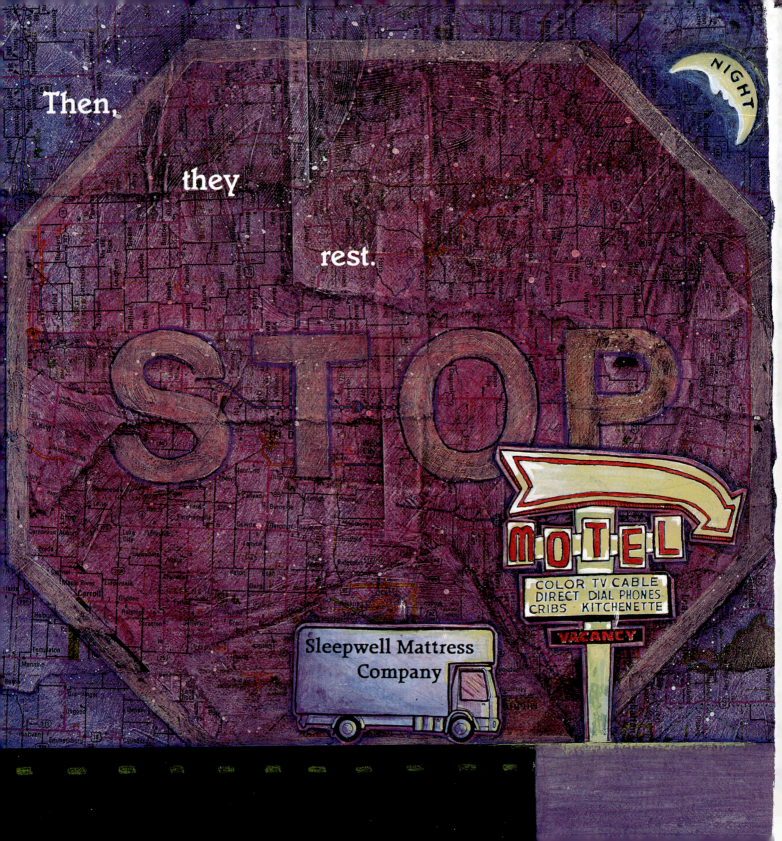

Then,

they

rest.